CHAPTER 1

SUMMER CAMP

It was Adam's first summer at camp.

He'd had a hard time talking Mom into letting him go.

"You've never been away from home before," she said. "Wait till you're a little older. Maybe next year."

But Dad was on Adam's side.

"Camp will be good for him," Dad said. "He'll make new friends. He'll have fun. And he'll learn a lot of new things."

Adam knew why Mom didn't want him to go. It was because he was deaf.

Mom was sure he couldn't do things the way other boys could. She was afraid the other boys would not be good to him. That they would make fun of him.

But Adam wanted to go more than anything. And this summer he didn't want to go to a special camp. One that was only for the disabled.

Adam begged and begged. At last Mom gave in.

"But you must write to us every day," she said. "And call us if things are not right."

"I will," Adam promised.

Adam liked camp a lot.

There were tall pine trees and fir trees. And there were green fields where wildflowers grew.

The boys slept on cots in big tents. They ate in another big tent. Sometimes they cooked over a campfire and ate

 outdoors. That was the most fun.

There were four other boys in Adam's tent. Kevin, Peter, Carlos, and Sam.

Kevin was the smallest. It was his first time at camp too. Adam could tell he was a little scared.

Peter had red hair and hundreds of brown freckles. He laughed a lot. He made the other boys laugh too. Adam really liked Peter.

Carlos had come to the United States just three years ago. He came from

Puerto Rico. Carlos was the only boy in his family. But he had seven sisters. All older.

The other boys teased Carlos about it. But he didn't mind. He was always in a good mood.

Adam thought he liked Carlos best.

Then there was Sam. Sam was bigger than the other boys. He was a little older too. He had been to the camp before.

Sam was not friendly to Adam. Adam could read lips. He knew Sam said a lot of bad things about him.

Adam tried not to let it hurt him. He knew that some people didn't know how to act around him. He understood this.

But Sam was rude. He made Adam feel like he didn't belong. As though he shouldn't be there.

Mr. Long was one of the camp leaders.
Adam like him a lot. He asked Adam to
teach the other boys some sign language.

"Cool!" the boys cried. All but Sam.

"Show me how to sign 'I'm hungry,' "
said Josh. He was always hungry.

Bill wanted to know how to sign "Happy birthday."

"How do I tell my sister to get lost?" asked one boy.

"You should teach that to Carlos," laughed Peter.

The other boys laughed too. All but Sam. Sam just glared at everyone. Even at Mr. Long.

One of the boys wanted to know how to tell jokes in sign language. Could Adam teach them?

Adam did. They made some mistakes. But some of the mistakes were funnier than the jokes.

Every night after dinner, the boys did camp chores. Then they sat around the fire. They had fun with sign language.

But Sam wouldn't even try.

"If you want to talk with your hands, go ahead," he sneered. "But don't think I'm going to do it."

CHAPTER

LEARNING
NEW THINGS

Dad had been right. Adam did make
friends. And he did learn a lot of new
things.

Adam learned to fish. One of the camp leaders took a picture of Adam holding his first fish. A ten-inch trout. Adam sent the picture home to Mom and Dad.

Dad wrote back, "I'll take you fishing when you get home. Maybe you'll catch a **real** fish!"

Adam and all the boys laughed at Dad's joke.

The camp leaders showed the boys how to put the fish on sticks. Then they cooked the fish over the fire. They tasted so good.

Adam learned to swim and row a boat. He learned to play some sports. He loved baseball.

Once Adam came in first in a race. Kevin signed, "You are a very good runner."

Adam felt good. He smiled and signed, "Thank you."

It was nice to be treated like all the other boys. By everyone but Sam. Adam tried not to let that bother him.

In a short time, all the other boys had learned some sign language. They had fun talking to Adam and each other.

One of the best things about camp was learning about nature. Adam loved the woods. He loved the tall trees. He loved the chipmunks that came into camp. The boys fed them peanuts and crackers.

One morning a chipmunk came into the tent where the boys ate. It climbed up on the table where Adam was eating breakfast. The chipmunk began to nibble on Adam's toast.

Before Adam knew what he was doing, he signed, "Hey, you. That's my toast!"

Everyone laughed hard. Even the camp leaders.

"That's a good one, Adam," said Mr. Long. "Signing to a chipmunk."

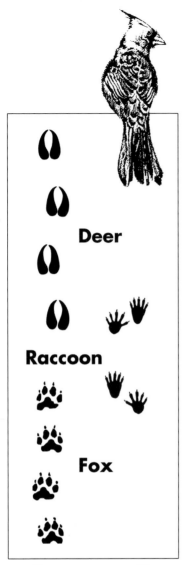

Deer

Raccoon

Fox

Adam laughed too. "It **was** pretty funny," he thought.

By the end of the first week, Adam could name over 20 birds. He knew the names of most of the wildflowers. He could tell the tracks of deer, raccoons, and foxes.

Adam was having a lot of fun at camp. But sometimes being deaf made him sad.

Like when Peter said, "You should have heard that owl last night. It was cool."

Or when the boys talked about hearing a

coyote howl.
Or when they
sang camp
songs around the
campfire. Adam
could only read
their lips.

Writing to Mom and Dad helped
some. Getting letters from them did too.

In one letter, Dad wrote, "It takes a
brave boy to do what you are doing. I
am very proud of you."

In Mom's
letters, she told
him over and over
how she missed
him and loved
him. He would
have so much to
tell them when he
got home.

In arts and crafts, he made a blue clay cat for Mom. Adam knew she would show it to all of her friends. Mom loved cats. They had three.

For Dad, he made a clay pencil holder for his desk. Adam was sure Dad would love it.

Adam had reason to feel even prouder. Mr. Long said to the class, "Adam did a very good job on his projects. Maybe he could help some of you."

Adam did help some of the boys. He was pleased that they asked him. Adam hoped he'd be able to come to camp next year too.

CHAPTER 3

IN THE WOODS

One day the camp leaders sent the boys out into the woods. Each group was to collect things for a nature study.

2 3

One group looked for rocks. One group collected insects.

Mr. Long sent Adam's group out to find leaves. They were learning the names of trees.

Mr. Long looked at Sam. "You are in charge, Sam. See that all the boys follow the rules."

Adam didn't like having Sam in charge. He was sure the other boys felt the same. He saw that Kevin was upset. Carlos just looked at Adam and shook his head.

"Don't be gone more than two hours," said Mr. Long. "Stay together. And stay on the marked trails."

"Don't worry, Mr. Long," said Sam. "I'll see that they do what I tell them." He looked right at Adam when he said it.

Adam walked along the trail beside Carlos. Kevin walked beside Peter. Sam walked a few feet ahead.

"Don't you guys forget that I'm in charge," Sam said.

"How could we forget?" Adam thought to himself. He wished Mr. Long had put someone else in charge.

But Adam enjoyed being in the woods. He like the way it smelled. And the way it felt. He couldn't hear the birds singing. But he liked looking at them.

They saw a mother flicker feeding her babies on a log. All the boys laughed.

"Those babies are all mouth," laughed Peter.

Adam couldn't hear the squirrels chattering. But he liked to watch them jump from limb to limb.

He couldn't hear the roaring of the creek. But he watched the water splash over the rocks. That was neat.

They found some nice maple leaves. And they found some dogwood and oak leaves. For a long time, they picked up leaves.

Suddenly Sam pointed to the ground. "Hey, guys. Look at this," he said. "It's a deer trail. Let's follow it."

"It goes way into the woods," said
Kevin.

"So?" said Sam. "I'm not scared."

"But we're supposed to stay on the
trails," said Peter. "That's what Mr. Long
told us."

"Well . . . ," Sam said. "That is a
trail."

"But Mr. Long told us . . . ," Peter
tried to say.

"Mr. Long will never know," said
Sam. "Not if you don't tell him. And you
better not."

"Come on, Sam," begged Carlos. "We
could get in trouble."

Adam signed, "Let's go back to camp."

"Who's in charge here anyway?" Sam
snapped. "You guys do what I say."

None of the boys made a move. They
just looked at each other.

Sam pulled Kevin's arm. "Now let's go," he ordered. "Follow me."

Slowly, Kevin, Carlos, Peter, and Adam followed Sam. Adam saw Kevin sniffling and wiping his nose on his sleeve. He knew Kevin was scared.

Adam was scared too. And he didn't want to get in trouble.

Deeper and deeper into the woods they went. After a while, Adam again signed, "Let's go back to camp."

"You just keep your hands in your pockets," said Sam.

He laughed loudly at his own joke. But no one else laughed.

Sam said, "Look. There are lots of deer tracks. Maybe we will see a deer. We'll go just a little farther. Then we'll go back to camp."

"We should go back now," said Carlos. "Mr. Long said not to be gone more than two hours."

"In a little while," Sam said.

The trail went up a little hill. At the top of the hill, the trail disappeared into some thick bushes.

"We can't get through that," said Peter.

"Right," agreed Carlos. "It's too thick."

Just then something darted out of the bushes. All the boys jumped.

Peter tripped. He rolled down the hill. "What—what was that?" he cried.

A big gray squirrel scurried up a nearby tree. From a limb, it scolded the boys. Adam tried to laugh, but he couldn't.

"Okay, you guys," said Sam. "We'll go back to camp now."

 CHAPTER

LOST!

But which way was camp? Everything looked the same. All the trees looked alike.

They tried to find their tracks. Maybe they could follow them back to camp. But the ground was too dry. The boys could not see any tracks.

Sam kept saying, "We'll be okay, you guys."

But an hour later, Adam knew they were really lost. So did Kevin, Carlos, and Peter.

Adam was sure Sam knew it too. But Sam kept saying, "We're fine. We're just turned around a little."

"I wish the sun was out," said Peter. "Maybe we could tell by that."

But it had become cloudy just before they left camp.

Adam was scared. He had never been this scared.

Adam had read stories about people who had been lost in the woods. He knew how cold it could get at night. And there were wild animals. There were bears and . . .

Adam tried to stop thinking about it.

"Hey, you guys," said Sam. "It's going to be all right. Don't panic. Just stay calm." He tried to smile a little. "Just stay cool."

But the boys knew Sam was really scared.

Carlos said, "I think we are just going around and around."

"Maybe we should stop walking," suggested Peter. "I think that's what you're supposed to do when you're lost."

"Right," said Carlos. "We should wait until someone finds us."

"We're not lost!" yelled Sam. "Now stop it!"

Sam really looked scared now. He had turned pale. His forehead was wet.

His hands were trembling. And he was walking very slowly.

Peter said, "I think we're getting farther away from camp."

"I think so too," said Kevin. His voice was shaky.

"We should have stayed on the trail," Carlos said. "We should have followed the rules."

At first Sam didn't say anything. Then he stopped. "All right. We'll stay right here for a while."

They all stood very still. No one said a word. Adam saw tears in Kevin's eyes.

It was scary. Adam knew the wind was blowing through the leaves. But he couldn't hear it. He saw a woodpecker pecking on a tree. But he couldn't hear the sound.

He wanted to cry. "Oh, if I could hear! If only I could hear!" he thought.

Suddenly Adam had an idea. He fell to the ground. He lay facedown. Then he spread his arms out wide.

"Are you crazy?" cried Sam. "What are you doing?"

Adam turned himself around and around on the ground.

"Get up from there right now!" Sam shouted.

The other boys stared at Adam.

"Are you okay?" asked Carlos.

Adam didn't answer. He pressed his hands hard against the ground.

Adam's fingers began to tingle. Harder and harder he pressed his hands.

The sound Adam was feeling got stronger. WHACK! WHACK! WHACK!

Adam's heart beat fast and hard. He knew what that sound was. That sound he was feeling with his hands.

Tonight they were having a big cookout. Someone back at camp was chopping wood.

Adam jumped to his feet. "Camp is that way," he signed.

"What did he say?" asked Sam.

"He said camp is that way," answered Carlos.

"You're crazy!" Sam yelled. "How can you tell that?"

Adam took off running as fast as he could. Carlos, Kevin, and Peter followed.

"Get back here!" called Sam.

None of the boys even looked back.

At last, Sam followed the other boys back to camp.

CHAPTER

CAMP HERO

It was late when the five boys got back to camp. Mr. Long stood in the middle of camp with his hands on his hips. He looked worried.

"What happened?" Mr. Long asked. "Where have you been?"

The boys were all puffing. No one could talk.

"You know you were not supposed to be gone that long," the camp leader said. "You didn't follow the rules."

"We—we got lost," Kevin panted.

"Lost!" cried Mr. Long. "How could you get lost? All the trails are marked."

Carlos, Kevin, Peter, and Adam looked at Sam. But no one said anything.

"Sam," said Mr. Long. "You were in charge. How could you get lost?"

Sam's face got red. He hung his head. "I—I saw a deer trail. I wanted to follow it," he said. "I thought we might see a deer."

"You knew better than that," Mr. Long said very loudly. "You never go off the trails. Only if an adult is with you."

The other camp leaders were looking at Sam. All the other boys were looking at him too. Sam looked down at the ground. He didn't say anything.

Adam couldn't help but feel a little sorry for Sam.

"It was Adam who found the way back," said Peter.

"Yes," said Kevin. "He saved us."

The boys were excited. They all began to talk at once. At last they were able to explain what Adam had done.

Everyone in the camp cheered.

"Right on!"

"Way to go, Adam!"

"Cool!"

Adam was really embarrassed. But he felt **so** good.

Mr. Long explained to the campers, "When one of the senses is gone, sometimes other senses grow stronger.

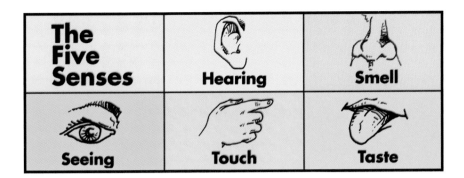

The Five Senses	Hearing	Smell
Seeing	Touch	Taste

Adam's sense of hearing is gone. But his sense of touch is strong. He was able to feel sound waves through his fingers. You boys were lucky to have Adam with you."

Carlos smiled. He slapped Adam on the back. "Adam not only talks with his hands, he hears with his hands," he said.

Adam saw Mr. Long walk over to Sam. He put his hand on Sam's shoulder. Adam couldn't tell what Mr. Long was saying. But he saw Sam smile a little.

Adam was glad.

It was time for dinner. And Adam was starved. He ate three hot dogs, three ears of corn, and two big helpings of salad. More than any of the other boys.

Adam was the camp hero. It was great. He could hardly wait to tell Mom and Dad. Wouldn't they be proud? Adam had never felt so good about himself.

But the best part of all came later. Just before they went to their tent, Sam came over to Adam. He put his face close to Adam's face. "I'm sorry," he said.

Adam nodded.

"Will—will you show me the sign for—for 'friends'?" asked Sam.

Adam smiled and signed "Friends."

Sam signed "Friends" back.

"That's the best sign of all," thought Adam.

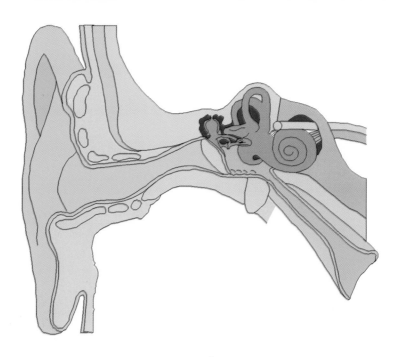

CHAPTER 6

DEAFNESS

Deafness can be caused by an illness or injury. Or a person may be born deaf. Often a person who is deaf is unable to talk.

Deaf people cannot talk because they cannot hear speech. They do not know how words sound.

Many deaf people can read lips. They communicate by reading lips and using sign language. But only with others who also know sign language.

We all use sign language in some ways. When we shake our heads, we are saying "No." When we nod our heads, we are saying "Yes."

We give a thumbs-up for something we think is good. A thumbs-down for something we don't like.

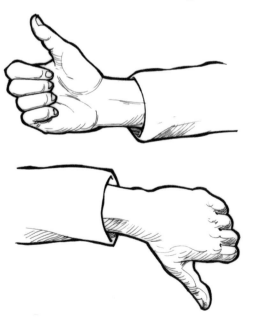

A raised hand in the classroom may mean "May I leave the room?"

We can even "talk" with our faces. Without making a sound. We smile to show we're happy. Or that something is funny. We glare when we're angry.

We can look sad. We can look surprised. We can show pain with our faces.

Indians used signs to talk with people who could not understand their language.

Hand signals are used in many ways. Signs are used in baseball and other sports. Railroad workers

use hand signals. A police officer or a crossing guard often holds up one hand. That tells people and cars to stop.

A music conductor uses his hands or a baton. He tells members of an orchestra or chorus how he wants them to play or sing. One signal may mean soft. Another, loud or fast or slow.

Before language was invented, all people must have used forms of sign language.

Even animals use signs to "talk." When a dog wags its tail, it's happy.

When it curls its upper lip and shows its teeth, it's angry. It may ask for food by sitting up and waving its paws.

A cat may beg for food by rubbing its body against its owner's legs. It may roll back and forth on its back to show pleasure. Sometimes a cat's ears lie flat on its head and it flips its tail. It's saying "Look out! I'm mad!"

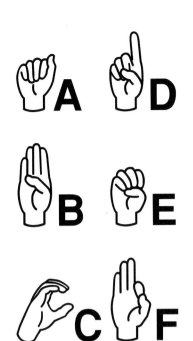

When a dog or cat wants to go outside, it may simply stand in front of the door.

Deaf people use over 1,500 signs. They also use finger spelling. They make letters of the alphabet by placing their fingers certain ways.

Over 250 years ago, the first school for the deaf was started. It was in Paris, France. It is thought that sign language and finger spelling also started there.

Helen Keller and Alexander Graham Bell

We think of Alexander Graham Bell
as the man who invented the telephone.
But he was also a teacher of the deaf. As
an adult, Bell's mother became deaf.
And he married a deaf woman who was
a student at his school.

Many people have overcome their deafness. And they have done things that seemed impossible.

Beethoven became totally deaf as a young man. Yet he went on to compose great music.

Helen Keller was deaf and blind. Until she was ten years old, she could talk only with sign language. But she wanted to learn to speak.

She took lessons from a teacher of the deaf. By the time she was 16, she could speak well enough to go to prep school. Then she went to college. She graduated with honors. Miss Keller wrote eight books.

Actresses Marlee Matlin and Amy Ecklund are deaf. Comic Kathy Buckley is also deaf.

An illness left Kitty O'Neil deaf when she was a baby. By the time she was 16, she had broken several high-diving records.

Kitty went on to become a movie stuntwoman. She raced motorcycles, cars, and speedboats. In 1976 she drove a rocket car over 600 mph. She was called the Fastest Woman on Earth.

When Kitty O'Neil was only 20 years old, her mother died. But Kitty never forgot what her mother told her when she was a child.

"Don't think of what you **can't** do. Think of what you **can** do."